Ellie's Doorstep

For Ellie, Lauren and Henry

A Beaver Book
Published by Arrow Books Limited
62-5 Chandos Place, London WC2N 4NW
An imprint of Century Hutchinson Ltd

London Melbourne Sydney Auckland
Johannesburg and agencies throughout the world

First published in 1988 by Hutchinson Children's Books
Beaver edition 1990

Set in Garamond by The Graphic Unit, London

Made and printed in Great Britain
by Scotprint, Musselburgh, Scotland

ISBN 0 09 960040 4

Alison Catley
Ellie's Doorstep

BEAVER BOOKS

In a sleepy town, in a sleepy street,
  At number twenty-four,
Lives a little girl aged three and a half
Named Ellie May Mary MaGraw.

Each morning she picks up the papers,
Then goes out on the doorstep to play.
Says, 'Hello,' to Sidney Spider,
'How are you feeling today?'

Mum says, 'Can't you play in the garden?
Can't you play here on the floor?'
But Ellie won't budge from the doorstep
Of number twenty-four.

For Ellie's doorstep is magic,
And nobody knows it but she.
If she closes her eyes and thinks very hard,
She can be anyone she wants to be.

First she opens her magical box
And searches for this and for that.
'Abracadabra! Alacazan!'
She's a wizard with black cloak and hat!

Next I'll be a teacher,' says Ellie,
'And, when I've counted to five,
I'll whisper my secretest magical spell
That makes all of my toys come alive.'

First Monkey picks up the trumpet,
And Teddy bangs on the drum,
Then they all start to play 'Old MacDonald' –
Rumpety! Tumpety! Tum!

Hey! Is that someone coming?
Mrs Ross from the top of the hill?
Oh, *not* Mrs Ross, she's bound to be cross.
Toys, you'd better be still.

'What is the password?' says Ellie.
Mrs Ross refuses to play:
'You here again! What a nuisance!
You'd better get out of my way.'

I can do magic,' says Ellie.
Mrs Ross pulls a very cross face,
'Oh, dear, you're always pretending.
Go pretend in some other place.'

'I'm *not* pretending,' says Ellie,
As she whispers a spell to the door.
And when Mrs Ross starts to complain,
All that comes out is, 'Eeyore!'

Mrs Ross pushes right past poor Ellie,
And in a second she's gone,
Without even knowing how lucky she is
That Ellie's spells don't last for long.

After lunch it's time for the postman.
'Is this number twenty-four?
For I want to deliver a letter
To Miss Ellie May Mary MaGraw.'

Ellie opens her very own letter.
'Oh good, Lucy is coming to play.
We'll dress up and pretend that we're grown-ups,
And take tea in a ladylike way.'

Ellie says, 'Let's cast a spell for a cake.
Abracadabra! Alacazan!
Oooh, this is nice, sugar and spice,
And a layer of pink marzipan.'

Lucy thinks Sidney is hungry.
'Sidney Spider, are you still awake?'
Sidney says he doesn't want any tea
But wouldn't mind a small piece of cake.

After they've played hunt the thimble,
Which turns into a marvellous game,
Lucy says that it's time she went home.
And now Ellie's alone once again.

Soon Ellie's toys are all sleepy,
So she sings them a lullaby
And reads them a very nice story
About a spider who lives in the sky.

Here's daddy home from the office.
'Who is this outside the door?
Is it a wizard? Is it a witch?
No, it's my Ellie May Mary MaGraw!'

After Dad's heard her adventures,
And her favourite story's been read . . .

A sleepy Ellie May Mary MaGraw
Is carried straight upstairs to bed.

In a sleepy town, in a sleepy street
Dreams Ellie May Mary MaGraw,
While Sidney Spider guards the doorstep
Of number twenty-four.

Other titles in the Beaver/Sparrow Picture Book series: